The Buried Moon

and other magical stories

Compiled by Vic Parker

First published in 2012 by Miles Kelly Publishing Ltd
Harding's Barn, Bardfield End Green, Thaxted, Essex, CM6 3PX, UK

2 4 6 8 10 9 7 5 3 1

Publishing Director Belinda Gallagher
Creative Director Jo Cowan
Editorial Director Rosie McGuire
Editor Carly Blake
Senior Designer Joe Jones
Editorial Assistant Lauren White
Production Manager Elizabeth Collins
Reprographics Anthony Cambray, Stephan Davis, Jennifer Hunt

ISBN 978-1-84810-574-4

Printed in China

British Library Cataloguing-in-Publication Data
A catalogue record for this book is available from the British Library

ACKNOWLEDGEMENTS
The publishers would like to thank the following artists who have contributed to this book:
Cover: Amerigo Pinelli at Advocate Art
Advocate Art: Alida Massari
The Bright Agency: Marcin Piwowarski, Tom Sperling
Marsela Hajdinjak

All other artwork from the Miles Kelly Artwork Bank

The publishers would like to thank the following sources for the use of their photographs:
Shutterstock: (page decorations) Dragana Francuski Tolimir
Dreamstime: (frames) Gordan

Every effort has been made to acknowledge the source and copyright holder of each picture.
Miles Kelly Publishing apologises for any unintentional errors or omissions.

Made with paper from a sustainable forest

www.mileskelly.net info@mileskelly.net

www.factsforprojects.com

Contents

The Council with the Munchkins

An extract from *The Wonderful Wizard of Oz*
by L Frank Baum

*Dorothy lives in a farmhouse in Kansas which is one day whisked
into the air by a tornado — with her and her little dog Toto inside!
It drops down into a wonderful land called Oz...*

DOROTHY SAT UP and noticed that the house was not moving. Nor was it dark, for the bright sunshine came in at the window, flooding the little room. She sprang from her bed and, with Toto at her heels, ran and opened the door.

The little girl gave a cry of amazement and looked about her, her eyes growing bigger and bigger at the wonderful sights she saw.

The cyclone had set the house down very gently – for a cyclone – in the midst of a country of marvellous beauty. There were lovely patches of grass all about, with stately trees bearing rich and luscious fruits. Banks of gorgeous flowers were on every hand, and birds with rare and brilliant plumage sang and fluttered in the trees and bushes. A little way off was a small brook, rushing and sparkling along between green banks, and murmuring in a voice very grateful to a little girl who had lived so long on the dry, grey prairies.

While she stood looking eagerly at the strange and beautiful sights, she noticed coming towards her a group of the queerest people she had ever seen. They were not as big as the grown folk she had always been used to, but neither were they very small. In fact, they seemed about as tall as Dorothy, who was a well-grown child for her age, although they were, so far as looks go, many years older.

Three were men and one a woman, and all were

oddly dressed. They wore round hats that rose to a small point a foot above their heads, with little bells around the brims that tinkled sweetly as they moved. The hats of the men were blue, the little woman's hat was white, and she wore a white gown that hung in pleats from her shoulders. Over it were sprinkled little stars that glistened in the sun like diamonds. The men were dressed in blue, of the same shade as their hats, and wore well-polished boots. The men, Dorothy thought, were about as old as Uncle Henry, for two of them had beards. But the little woman was doubtless much older. Her face was covered with wrinkles, her hair was nearly white, and she walked rather stiffly.

When these people drew near the house where Dorothy was standing in the doorway, they paused and whispered among themselves, as if afraid to come farther. But the little old woman walked up to

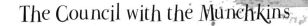

Dorothy, made a low bow and said, in a sweet voice: "You are welcome, most noble Sorceress, to the land of the Munchkins. We are so grateful to you for having killed the Wicked Witch of the East, and for setting our people free from bondage."

Dorothy listened to this speech with wonder. What could the little woman possibly mean by calling her a sorceress, and saying she had killed the Wicked Witch of the East? Dorothy was an innocent, harmless little girl, who had been carried by a cyclone many miles from home, and she knew very well that she had never killed anything in all her life.

But the little woman evidently expected her to answer, so Dorothy said, with hesitation, "You are very kind, but there must be some mistake. I have not killed anything."

"Your house did, anyway," replied the little old woman, with a laugh, "and that is the same thing."

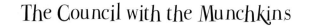

She pointed to the
corner of the house.

"There are her two feet, still sticking out from
under a block of wood."

Dorothy looked, and gave a little cry of fright.
There, indeed, just under the corner of the great
beam the house rested on, two feet were sticking
out, shod in silver shoes with pointed toes.

"Oh, dear! Oh, dear!" cried Dorothy, clasping her
hands together in great dismay. "The house must

have fallen on her. Whatever shall we do?"

"There is nothing to be done," said the little woman calmly.

"But who was she?" asked Dorothy.

"She was the Wicked Witch of the East, as I said," answered the little woman. "She has held all the Munchkins in bondage for many years, making them slave for her night and day. Now they are all set free, and are grateful to you for the favour."

"Who are the Munchkins?" enquired Dorothy.

"They are the people who live in this land of the East where the Wicked Witch ruled."

"Are you a Munchkin?" asked Dorothy.

"No, but I am their friend, although I live in the land of the North. When they discovered that the Witch of the East was dead the Munchkins sent a messenger to me. I am the Witch of the North."

"Gracious!" cried Dorothy. "Are you a real witch?"

"Yes, indeed," answered the little woman. "But I am a good witch, and the people love me. I am not as powerful as the Wicked Witch was who ruled here, or I should have set the people free myself."

"But I thought all witches were wicked," said the girl, who was half frightened at facing a real witch.

"Oh, no. There were only four witches in all of Oz, and two of them, those who live in the North and the South, are good. I know this is true, for I am one of them. Those who dwelled in the East and the West were wicked witches, but now that you have killed one of them, there is but one Wicked Witch in all of Oz – the one who lives in the West."

"But," said Dorothy, after a moment's thought, "Aunt Em has told me that the witches were all dead – years and years ago."

"Who is Aunt Em?" enquired the little old woman.

"She is my aunt and she lives in Kansas – where I came from."

The Witch of the North seemed to think for a time. Then she said, "I do not know where Kansas is, for I have never heard of that country mentioned before. Tell me, is it a civilised country?"

"Oh, yes," replied Dorothy.

"Then that accounts for it. In the civilised countries I believe there are no witches left, nor wizards, sorceresses or magicians. The Land of Oz has never been civilised, for we are cut off from all the rest of the world. Therefore we still have witches and wizards among us."

"Who are the wizards?" asked Dorothy.

"Oz himself is the Great Wizard," answered the Witch. "He is more powerful than all the rest of us together. He lives in the City of Emeralds."

Just then the Munchkins, who had been standing silently by, gave a shout and pointed to the corner of the house where the Wicked Witch had been lying.

"What is it?" asked the little old woman. The feet of the dead Witch had disappeared and nothing was left but the silver shoes.

"She was so old," explained the Witch of the

North, "that she dried up quickly in the sun. That is the end of her. But the silver shoes are yours." She reached down and picked up the shoes, and after shaking the dust out of them gave them to Dorothy.

"The Witch of the East was proud of those shoes," said one of the Munchkins, "and there is charm connected with them, but what it is we never knew."

Dorothy took the shoes into the house. Then she came out to the Munchkins and said: "I must get back to my aunt and uncle, for I am sure they will worry about me. Can you help me find my way?"

The Munchkins and the Witch looked at one another and at Dorothy, and shook their heads.

"At the East, not far from here," said one, "there is a great desert, and none could live to cross it."

"It is the same at the South," said another. "The South is the country of the Quadlings."

"I am told," said the third man, "that it is the same at the West. And that country, where the Winkies live, is ruled by the Wicked Witch of the West, who

would make you her slave if you passed her way."

"The North is my home," said the old lady, "and at its edge is the same great desert that surrounds this Land of Oz. I'm afraid you will have to live with us."

Dorothy began to sob at this, for she felt lonely among all these strange people. Her tears seemed to grieve the kind-hearted Munchkins, for they took out their handkerchiefs and began to weep also. As for the little old woman, she took off her cap and balanced the point on the end of her nose, while she counted, "One, two, three". At once the cap changed to a slate, on which was written:

LET DOROTHY GO TO THE CITY OF EMERALDS.

The little old woman took the slate from her nose, and having read the words on it, asked, "Is your name Dorothy, my dear?"

"Yes," answered the child, drying her tears.

"Then you must go to the City of Emeralds. Perhaps Oz will help you."

"Where is this city?" asked Dorothy.

"It is exactly in the centre of the country, and is ruled by Oz, the Great Wizard I told you of."

"Is he a good man?" enquired the girl anxiously.

"He is a good Wizard. Whether he is a man or not I cannot tell, for I have never seen him."

"How can I get there?" asked Dorothy.

"You must walk. It is a long journey, through a country that is sometimes pleasant and sometimes dark and terrible. However, I will use all the magic arts I know of to keep you from harm."

"Won't you go with me?" pleaded the girl, who had begun to look upon the little old woman as her only friend.

"No, I cannot do that," she replied, "but I will give you my kiss, and no one will dare injure a person who has been kissed by the Witch of the North."

She came close to Dorothy and kissed her gently on the forehead. Where her lips touched the girl they left a round, shining mark.

"The road to the City of Emeralds is paved with yellow brick," said the Witch, "so you cannot miss it. When you get to Oz do not be afraid of him. Tell your story and ask him to help you. Goodbye, my dear."

The three Munchkins wished her a pleasant journey, then walked away through the trees. The Witch gave Dorothy a nod, whirled around on her left heel three times, and disappeared.

But Dorothy, knowing her to be a witch, had expected her to disappear in just that way, and was not surprised in the least.

Do You Believe in Fairies?

An extract from Peter Pan by J M Barrie

The home of the Darling children — Wendy, John and Michael — is often visited by a flying boy called Peter Pan. One night, Peter whisks the children to his home — Neverland — so Wendy can mother his gang, the Lost Boys. But Neverland is a dangerous place and, unfortunately, Wendy and her brothers are captured by Captain Hook and his evil band of pirates. Peter's best friend, a mischievous fairy called Tinker Bell, comes to break the bad news to him…

PETER SLEPT ON. The light guttered and went out, leaving the tenement in darkness, but still he slept. It must have been not less than ten o'clock, when he sat up in his bed, wakened by a soft, cautious tapping on the door of his tree.

Soft and cautious, but in that stillness it was

sinister. Peter felt for his dagger till his hand gripped it. Then he spoke: "Who is that?"

For a long time there was no answer, but then he heard the knock again.

"Who are you?"

No answer.

Peter was thrilled, and he loved being thrilled. In two strides he reached the door.

"I won't open unless you speak," Peter cried. Then at last the visitor spoke, in a bell-like voice. "Let me in, Peter."

It was Tink, and quickly he unbarred to her. She flew in excitedly, her face flushed and her dress stained with mud.

"What is it?"

"Oh, you could never guess!" she cried, and offered him three guesses.

"Out with it!" he shouted, and in one ungrammatical sentence, as long as the ribbons that magicians pull from their mouths, she told of the capture of Wendy and the boys.

Peter's heart bobbed up and down as he listened. Wendy bound, and on the pirate ship – she who loved everything to be just so!

"I'll rescue her!" he cried, leaping at his weapons. As he leaped he thought of something he could do to please her. He could take his medicine.

His hand closed on the fatal draught.

"No!" shrieked Tinker Bell, who had heard Hook mutter about his deed as he sped through the forest.

"Why not?"

"It is poisoned."

"Poisoned? Who could have poisoned it?"

"Hook."

"Don't be silly. How indeed could Hook have got

down here?"

Alas, Tinker Bell could not explain this. Nevertheless Hook's words had left no room for doubt. The cup was poisoned.

"Besides," said Peter, quite believing himself, "I never fell asleep."

He raised the cup. No time for words now, time for deeds, and with one of her lightning movements Tink got between his lips and the draught, and drained it to the dregs.

"Why, Tink, how dare you drink my medicine?"

But she did not answer. Already she was reeling in the air.

"What is the matter with you?" cried Peter, suddenly afraid.

"It was poisoned, Peter," she told him softly, "and now I am going to be dead."

"O Tink, did you drink it to save me?"

"Yes."

"But why, Tink?"

19

Her wings would scarcely carry her now, but in reply she alighted on his shoulder and gave his nose a loving bite. She whispered in his ear, "You silly ass," and then, tottering to her chamber, laid on the bed.

His head almost filled the fourth wall of her little room as he knelt near her in distress. Every moment her light was growing fainter, and he knew that if it went out she would be no more. She liked his tears so much that she put out her finger and let them run over it.

Her voice was so low that at first he could not make out what she said. Then he made it out. She was saying that she thought she could get well again if children believed in fairies.

There were no children there, and it was night time, but Peter addressed all who might be dreaming of the Neverland, and who were therefore near to him: boys and girls everywhere.

"Do you believe in fairies?" he cried.

Tink sat up in bed almost briskly to listen intently to her fate.

She fancied she heard answers in the affirmative, and then again she wasn't sure.

"What do you think?" she asked Peter.

"If you believe," he shouted to them, "clap your hands – don't let Tink die."

Many clapped.

Some didn't.

A few beastly ones hissed.

The clapping stopped suddenly, as if countless mothers had rushed to their children's bedrooms to see what on earth was happening, but already Tink was saved. Her voice grew strong, then she popped out of bed, then she was flashing through the room more merry and impudent than ever. She never thought of thanking those who believed, but she would have like to get at the ones who had hissed.

"And now to rescue Wendy!"

Shipwreck on Lilliput

An extract from *Gulliver's Travels*
by Jonathan Swift, adapted by John Lang

*Lemuel Gulliver is a young surgeon who falls on hard times. He takes
work on board ships making long sea voyages to strange, distant lands. On
one such journey, far from home, a terrible storm wrecks his ship, washing
away all the crew and leaving Gulliver at the mercy of the waves…*

GULLIVER SWAM till no strength or feeling
was left in his arms and legs. He swam
bravely, his breath coming in sobs, his eyes blinded

with the salt seas that broke over his head. Still he struggled on, until at last, in a part where the wind seemed to have less force, on letting down his legs he found that he was within his depth. But the shore shelved so gradually that for nearly a mile he had to wade wearily through shallow water, till, almost fainting with fatigue, he reached dry land.

By this time darkness was coming on, and there were no signs of houses or of people. He staggered forward but a little distance, and then, on the short, soft turf, sank down exhausted and slept.

When he woke, the sun was shining. He tried to rise, but not by any means could he stir hand or foot. Gulliver had slept lying on his back, and now he found that his arms and legs were tightly fastened

to the ground. Across his body were numbers of thin but strong cords, and even his hair, which was very long, was pegged down so securely that he could not turn his head.

All round about him there was a confused sound of voices, but he could see nothing except the sky, and the sun shone so hot and fierce into his eyes that he could scarcely keep them open.

Soon he felt something come gently up his left leg, and forward on to his breast almost to his chin. Looking down as much as possible, he saw standing there a very little man, not more than six inches high, armed with a bow and arrows.

Then many more small men began to swarm over him. Gulliver let out such a roar of wonder and fright that they all turned and ran. But very quickly the little people came back again. This time, with a great struggle Gulliver managed to break the cords that fastened his left arm, and at the same time, by a violent wrench that hurt him dreadfully, he slightly loosened the strings that fastened his hair, so that he was able to turn his head a little to one side. But the little men were too quick for him, and got out of reach before he could catch any of them.

Then he heard a great shouting, followed by a shrill little voice that called sharply, "Tolgo phonac," and immediately, arrows like needles were shot into his hand, and another volley struck him in the face. Poor Gulliver covered his face with his hand, and lay groaning with pain.

Again he struggled to get loose. But the harder he fought for freedom, the more the little men shot arrows into him, and some of them even tried to run their spears into his sides.

When he found that the more he struggled the more he was hurt, Gulliver lay still, thinking to himself that at night at least, now that his left hand was free, he could get rid of the rest of his bonds. As soon as the little people saw that he struggled no more, they ceased shooting at him, but he knew from the increasing sound of voices that more and more of the little soldiers were coming round him.

A few yards from him, on the right, he heard a continued sound of hammering, and on turning his head to that side as far as the strings would let him, he saw that a small wooden stage was being built. On to this, when it was finished, there climbed by ladders four men, and one of them (who seemed to be a very important person) immediately gave an order. At once about fifty of the soldiers ran forward and cut the strings that tied Gulliver's hair on the left side, so that he could turn his head to the right.

Then the person began to make a long speech, not one word of which could Gulliver understand, but it seemed to him that sometimes the little man threatened and sometimes made offers of kindness.

As well as he could, Gulliver made signs that he submitted. Then, feeling by this time faint with hunger, he pointed with his fingers many times to his mouth, to show that he wanted something to eat.

They understood him very well. Several ladders were put against Gulliver's sides, and about a hundred little people climbed up and carried to his mouth all kinds of bread and meat. There were things shaped like legs, and shoulders, and saddles of mutton. Very good they were, Gulliver thought, but very small, no bigger than a lark's wing, and the loaves of bread were about the size of bullets, so that he could take several at a mouthful. The people wondered greatly at the amount that he ate.

When he signed that he was thirsty, they slung up two of their biggest casks of wine, and having rolled them forward to his hand they knocked out the heads of the casks. Gulliver drank them both and asked for more, for they held only about a small tumblerful each. But there was no more to be had.

As the small people walked to and fro over his body, Gulliver was sorely tempted to seize forty or fifty of them and dash them on the ground, and then to make a further struggle for liberty. But the pain he had already suffered from their arrows made him think better of it, and he wisely lay quiet.

Soon another small man, who from his brilliant uniform seemed to be an officer of very high rank, marched with some others on to Gulliver's chest and held up to his eyes a paper which Gulliver understood to be an order from the king of the country. The officer made a long speech, often pointing towards something a long way off, and told him that he was to be taken as a prisoner to the city, the capital of the country.

The city was not reached till the following day, whereupon Gulliver was brought to a large building. Inside the building the king's blacksmiths fastened many chains, which they then brought through one of these little windows and padlocked round Gulliver's left ankle.

Gulliver found that he could easily creep through the door, and that there was room inside to lie down. He could also get a little exercise by walking backwards and forwards outside. Then the king gave orders that food should be brought for Gulliver, twenty little carts full, and ten of wine, and he and his courtiers, all covered with gold and silver, stood and watched him eating. After the king had gone, the people of the city crowded round, and some of them began to behave badly, one man even going so far as to shoot an arrow at Gulliver which was not far from putting out one of his eyes. But the officer in command of the soldiers ordered his men to bind and push six of the worst behaved within reach of Gulliver, who at once seized five of them and put them in his coat pocket. The sixth he held up to his mouth and made as if he meant to eat him, whereupon the wretched

little creature shrieked aloud with terror, and when
Gulliver took out his knife, all the people, even the
soldiers, were dreadfully alarmed. But Gulliver only
cut the man's bonds and let him run away, which he
did in a great hurry. And when he took the others
out of his pocket, one by one, and treated them in
the same way, the crowd began to laugh.

After that the people always behaved very well to
Gulliver, and he became a great favourite. From all
over the kingdom crowds flocked to see the Great
Man Mountain.

The Buried Moon

From *Tales of Wonder Every Child Should Know*
by Kate Douglas Wiggin and
Nora Archibald Smith

LONG AGO, the Carland was all in bogs, great pools of black water, and creeping trickles of green water, and squishy mools which squirted when you stepped on them. The Moon up yonder shone just as she does now, and when she shone she lighted up the bogpools, so that one could walk about almost as safe as in the day. But when she didn't shine, out came the Things that dwelled in the darkness and went about seeking to do evil and harm – Bogles and Crawling Horrors, all came out when the Moon didn't shine.

The Buried Moon

Well, the Moon heard of this, and being kind and good – as she surely is, shining for us in the night instead of taking her natural rest – she was main troubled. "I'll see for myself, I will," said she, "maybe it's not so bad as folks make out."

Sure enough, at the month's end down she stepped, wrapped up in a black cloak, and a black hood over her yellow shining hair. Straight she went to the bog edge and looked about her. Water here and water there, waving tussocks and trembling mools, and great black snags all twisted and bent. Before her all was dark – dark but for the glimmer of the stars in the pools, and the light that came from her own white feet, stealing out of her black cloak.

The Moon drew her cloak faster about her and trembled, but she wouldn't go back without seeing all there was to be seen, so on she went, stepping as light as the wind in summer from tuft to tuft between the muddy, gurgling water holes. Just as she came near a big black pool her foot slipped and she was nigh tumbling in. She grabbed with both hands at a snag nearby, to steady herself with, but as she touched it, it twined itself round her wrists, like a pair of handcuffs, and gripped her so that she couldn't move. She pulled and twisted and fought, but it was no good. She was fast, and must stay fast.

Presently as she stood trembling in the dark, wondering if help would come, she heard something calling in the distance, calling, calling, and then dying away with a sob, till the marshes were full of this pitiful crying sound. Then she heard steps floundering along, squishing in the mud and slipping on the tufts, and through the darkness she saw a white face with great feared eyes.

It was a man strayed in the bogs. Mazed with fear he struggled on toward the flickering light that looked like help and safety. And when the poor Moon saw that he was coming nigher and nigher to the deep hole, farther and farther from the path, she was so mad and so sorry that she struggled and fought and pulled harder than ever. And though she couldn't get loose she twisted and turned, till her black hood fell back off her shining yellow hair, and the beautiful light that came from it drove away the darkness.

Oh, but the man cried with joy to see the light

again. And at once all evil things fled back into the dark corners, for they cannot abide the light. So he could see where he was, and where the path was, and how he could get out of the marsh. And he was in such haste to get away from the Quicks, and Bogles, and Things that dwelled there, that he scarce looked at the brave light that came from the beautiful shining yellow hair, streaming out over the black cloak and falling to the water at his feet. And the Moon herself was so taken up with saving him, and with rejoicing that he was back on the right path, that she clean forgot that she needed help herself, and that she was held fast by the black snag.

So off he went, spent and gasping, and stumbling and sobbing with joy, flying for his life out of the terrible bogs. Then it came over the Moon, she would main like to go with him. So she pulled and fought as if she were mad, till she fell on her knees, spent with tugging, at the foot of the snag. And as she lay there, gasping for breath, the black hood fell

forward over her head. So out went the blessed
Light and back came the darkness, with all its Evil
Things, with a screech and a howl. They came
crowding round her, mocking and snatching and
beating, shrieking with rage and spite, and swearing
and snarling, for they knew her for their old enemy,
that drove them back into the corners, and kept
them from working their wicked wills.

They caught hold of her, with horrid bony fingers,
and laid her deep in the water at the foot of the snag.
And the Bogles fetched a strange big stone and
rolled it on top of her, to keep her from rising. And
they told two of the Will-o-the-wykes to take turns
in watching on the black snag, to see that she lay safe
and still, and couldn't get out to spoil their sport.
And there lay the poor Moon, dead and buried in
the bog till someone would set her loose – and
who'd know where to look for her?

Well, the days passed, and it was the time for the
new Moon's coming, and the folk looked about, for

the Moon was a good friend to the marsh folk, and they were main glad when the dark time was gone, and the paths were safe again, and the Evil Things were driven back by the blessed Light into the darkness and the waterholes.

But days and days passed, and the new Moon never came, and the nights were aye dark, and the Evil Things were worse than ever. And still the days went on, and the new Moon never came. Naturally the poor folk were strangely feared and mazed.

One day, as they sat in the inn, a man from the far end of the bog lands was smoking and listening to the talk about the Moon, when all at once he sat up and slapped his knee. "I'd clean forgot, but I reckon I kens where the Moon be!" he said, and he told them of how he was lost in the bogs, and how, when he was nigh dead with fright, the light shone out, and he found the path and got home safe.

So come the next night in the darklings, out they went all together, everyone feeling, thou may'st reckon, main feared and creepy. And they stumbled and stottered along the paths into the midst of the bogs. They saw naught, though they heard sighings and flutterings in their ears, and felt cold wet fingers touching them, but all together, looking around, while they came nigh to the pool beside the great snag, where the Moon lay buried. And all at once they stopped, quaking and mazed and skeery, for there was the great stone, half in, half out of the water, for all the world like a strange big coffin, and at the head was the black snag, stretching out its two arms in a dark gruesome cross, and on it a tiddy light flickered, like a dying candle. And they all knelt down in the mud, and said, "Our Lord".

Then they went nigher, and took hold of the big stone, and shoved it up, and afterward they said that for one minute they saw a strange and beautiful face looking up at them glad-like out of the black water, but the Light came so quick and so white and shining, that they stepped back mazed with it, and

the very next minute, when they could see again, there was the full Moon in the sky, bright and beautiful and kind as ever, shining and smiling down at them, and making the bogs and the paths as clear as day, and stealing into the very corners, as though she'd have driven the darkness and the Bogles clean away if she could.